THE LONGEST

HAIR

EVER

By Cathy Mahalik

Order this book online at www.trafford.com
or email orders@trafford.com

Most Trafford titles are also available at major online book retailers.

 www.trafford.com

North America & international
toll-free: 844 688 6899 (USA & Canada)
fax: 812 355 4082

Our mission is to efficiently provide the world's finest, most comprehensive book publishing service, enabling every author to experience success. To find out how to publish your book, your way, and have it available worldwide, visit us online at www.trafford.com

Because of the dynamic nature of the Internet, any web addresses or links contained in this book may have changed since publication and may no longer be valid. The views expressed in this work are solely those of the author and do not necessarily reflect the views of the publisher, and the publisher hereby disclaims any responsibility for them.

ISBN: 978-1-4269-4396-6 (sc)
        978-1-4669-2481-9 (e)

Library of Congress Control Number: 2011901124

Print information available on the last page.

Trafford rev. 11/05/2021

This book is dedicated to my three wonderful children, Shannon, Danielle, and Michael. Special thanks to Danielle, for being my inspiration. The day she looked into a mirror and made a wish, a story was born.

I would also like to thank my Dad, Bruce Grisi, who helped me with this book in so many ways.

One day I was looking in the mirror wishing I had longer hair than my sister.

Then the strangest thing happened.

My wish came true!

Right before my eyes
my hair started growing!

It grew past
my feet and dragged on the
floor behind me as I walked.
I had to show my family
right away.

I raced into the living room where they were watching TV. Their mouths flew open.

"That's the longest hair ever!"
"Yes", I answered proudly.

They couldn't believe their eyes! "Wow!" my sister cried.

"Isn't it wonderful?"

Mom decided to braid my long hair to keep it from getting knots.

It took her an hour!

The next day on the bus going to school, my hair blew out the window.

Screech!

Two cars nearly crashed
because people were staring
at my hair.

In school I had to roll up my hair because some kids tripped on it.

They really should have watched where they were going.

My teacher, Miss Emma, helped me put it up with pencils.

But at recess, I pulled out the pencils and let my hair down to play jump rope.

Everyone lined up for a turn.

"Your hair is
the best!" they all shouted.

When I got home, mom was getting ready to mop the floor. "I'll do it!" I said. I quickly pulled my braid out. Then I dipped my hair in some soapy water

and walked all across the floor until it sparkled.

"Beautiful job!" Mom said.

"The floor is clean but now your hair is dirty".

I decided to take a shower. It was hard to keep my hair from slithering down the drain.

After, Mom had to comb out the knots. "Ouch!" I cried. "You're hurting me!"

"I'm sorry" Mom said, "but this hair is just too long! How about if I trim it a bit?"

"Well, okay," I agreed.

Mom trimmed my hair to the back of my knees. I was so glad to get rid of those knots!

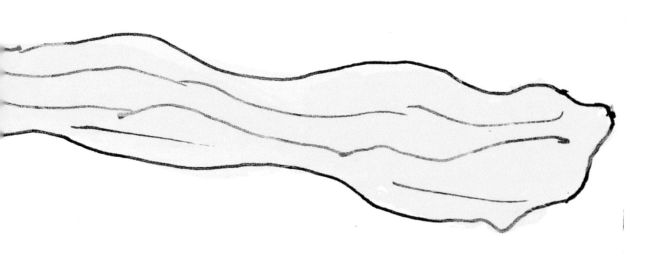

I plopped into bed but I couldn't go to sleep. My hair kept getting in my face.

I tried to get it out by tying it in a bow.

When I woke up in the morning, I was surprised to find my hair had grown overnight, as if Mom had never cut it!

This continued for a week. Mom cut it each night and by morning it would be back.

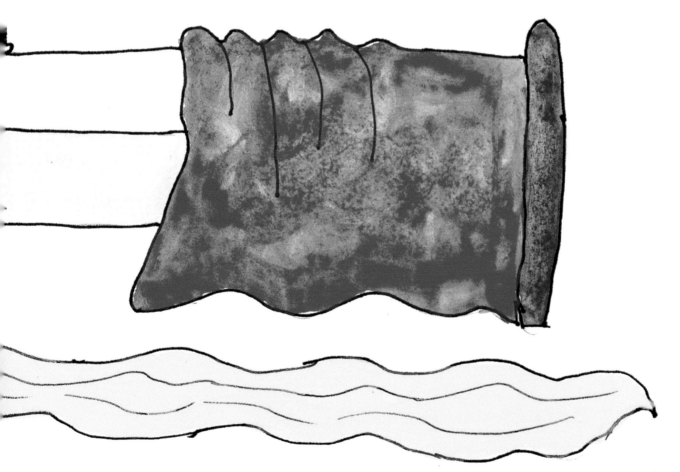

I didn't know what to do. Having the longest hair ever was not so wonderful anymore.

I had an idea. I looked in the mirror and wished my hair were back the way it used to be. *It worked!* Just as strange

as it all began. I watched as my hair got shorter and shorter. It stopped just below my shoulders.

"Perfect!" I shouted.

And it was . . .

perfect

to be just me again.

Printed in the United States
by Baker & Taylor Publisher Services